D1214504

Ask your booksellers for all the books in The Rumpoles and the Barleys series by Karen Hunt.

The Rumpoles and the Barleys
A Picnic with the Barleys

For Katya, Harrison, and Max

A Picnic with the Barleys

Copyright © 1989 by Karen Hunt

Published by Harvest House Publishers
Eugene, Oregon 97402
www.harvesthousepublishers.com
ISBN-13: 978-0-7369-2173-2
ISBN-10: 0-7369-2173-7

Design and production by Dugan Design Group, Bloomington, Minnesota

All rights reserved. No portion of this book may be reproduced, stored in a retrieval system, or transmitted in any form or by any means—electronic, mechanical, digital, photocopy, recording, or any other—except for brief quotations in printed reviews, without the prior permission of the publisher.

Printed in China

08 09 10 11 12 13 14 15 / LP / 10 9 8 7 6 5 4 3 2 1

A Picnic
WITH
The Barleys

Karen Hunt

HARVEST HOUSE PUBLISHERS

EUGENE, OREGON

It was a glorious, sunshiny day, just right for a picnic in the country. The windows of the Rumpole Mansion were open wide to let in the fragrance from the gardens below and the nearby fields.

Way up in the attic of the mansion lived the Rumpole mice. The two little mouse children, Eustace and Prunella, peeked out of the tip-top window, their mouse noses twitching with excitement.

"Hurry now," called Papa Rumpole. "The Barleys and all their country friends will be waiting." The little mouse noses disappeared in a flash.

At last they were ready to go. Eustace and Prunella looked over the windowsill of their tiny bedroom window. Samuel the cat was busy chasing butterflies in the garden.

Down the drainpipe they slid. Prunella held tightly to her new pink parasol. It had been a birthday present and was very special.

 I nside, Mama Rumpole took a last look in the mirror as she
tied her new summer bonnet.

"What a pretty picture you make, my dear," said Papa
Rumpole. "As pretty as the day we met." He gave her a little
squeeze. "Oh, nonsense!" she said, blushing.

Mama and Papa Rumpole crept down the back stairs, being careful not to spill the lemonade and being VERY careful not to be seen. Living in the Rumpole Mansion wasn't always easy.

What a happy scamper! Past the nodding daffodils and tulips of the home garden. Past the lilac hedges and wild roses. On and on to the shady pathway leading down to the river.

"Come closer, children," said Papa Rumpole when they stopped to rest beneath a leafy branch. "Before we go any further, I must warn you not to go near the dark bog where Weasel lives. See—there it is beyond the clover field."

"No indeed," said Mama Rumpole fearfully. "We…wea…weasels just don't like us very much." She shivered and gave each of the children a quick hug.

"We'll be *very* careful," promised Eustace solemnly.

"Very careful," echoed Prunella.

S oon happy squeaks and squeals could be heard among the clover blossoms and down by the river.

"Hello, hello," called all the Barleys, their country friends.
"Well, hello there!" called all the jolly McAcorns.
"Pleased to meet you," beamed the Oatleys and the Wheatkins.

The Rumpole mice felt just a little shy in the company of
so many lively country folk, and Mama Rumpole wondered
if she wasn't just a trifle overdressed. But everyone was so
friendly that they were soon put at ease.

"There's Dagwood!" Eustace and Prunella cried, happy
to see their good friend. He introduced them to all the other
little mice. Then he picked up his fishing pole and headed for
the river.

"See you later," Dagwood called with a flourish of his cap.
"Don't want any noisy mice around to scare the fish."

With "oohs" and "aahs" Prunella's new friends crowded around
and begged to hold her parasol. Especially Cordelia.
She was big and bold and grabby and wore a tattered lavender
pinafore. Prunella decided not to give her a turn.

tug-o'-war...

Soon all the little mice were playing hide-and-seek...

and follow the leader. The two Rumpole children had never had such a fine time.

All at once Prunella let out a dreadful cry. "My parasol! It's gone!"
And so it was. Nowhere across the clover field nor by the riverbank
could it be seen.

Quickly Eustace looked around. Where was that parasol? Out of
the corner of his eye, he saw a bit of pink disappear among the trees of
the dark bog. He also saw a bit of lavender pinafore.

Eustace ran. His little feet flew. Then he stopped—fast.
He remembered what Papa had said.
"Cordelia," he called breathlessly. "Come back…weasels!"

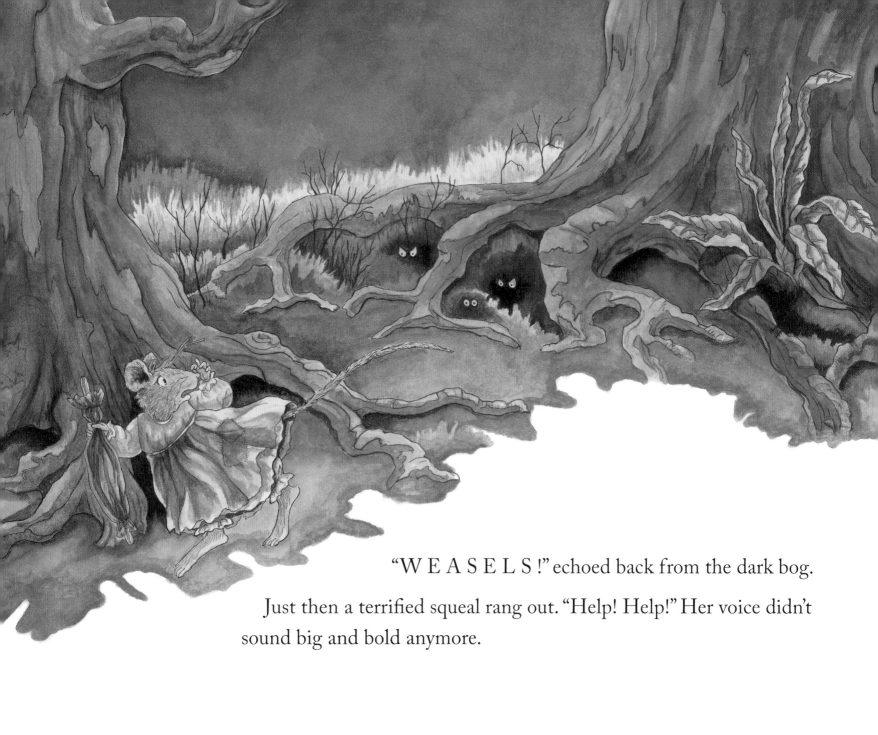

"W E A S E L S !" echoed back from the dark bog.

Just then a terrified squeal rang out. "Help! Help!" Her voice didn't sound big and bold anymore.

Suddenly from the riverbank appeared a fishing pole and a
familiar cap. Tossing his cap to Eustace for safekeeping, Dagwood
landed with a mighty leap on a twisty branch floating in the bog.
Hop! Dagwood balanced on the next branch. And the next.
"Help!" came another cry.

With a final leap Dagwood landed very near to a muddy, oozy, smelly lavender dress attached to a pink parasol. "Gulp...glub...slurp," came from somewhere under the sticky mess. Dagwood grabbed the parasol and pulled hard.

At that instant two glittery, hungry eyes shone out of the darkness.

It's a WEASEL!

With a desperate yank Dagwood pulled Cordelia out of the bog and onto the branch beside him.

Then IT jumped out at Dagwood. Fighting courageously, the bold
field mouse gave a mighty jab with his fishing pole. Down the weasel
fell into the muddy goo.

At the same moment something pink slithered and slid beneath
the water. With a little "plop" Prunella's lovely parasol disappeared.
Dagwood grabbed Cordelia's dirty paw and back they flew over
the twigs and branches of the dark bog to the safety of the riverbank.

What hugs and happy cries greeted them there! All the little mice crowded around their hero.

"Oh, it was nothing," Dagwood declared, straightening his cap. "Any decent mouse would have done the same."

"Well, I don't think it was nothing," said Prunella shyly.

Poor Cordelia was quite forgotten. She hung her head and blew her nose into her pinafore.

Then she felt a soft kiss and a little paw on her arm.

"I'm sorry I didn't share my parasol with you," said Prunella "And I don't mind that you lost it. Let's forgive each other and be friends."

Later, after everyone had eaten and the moon was up,
Papa Barley got out his fiddle and played a lively tune. What a happy
frolic as they danced and sang and retold the story of brave
Dagwood's daring rescue.

As they looked up at the twinkling stars, Papa Barley changed to a soft, sweet tune and everyone became quiet and thoughtful. Then he turned to Prunella and Cordelia and said kindly, "Remember, it is also brave to say 'sorry' and to forgive."

O Lord, You are so good and kind, so ready to forgive; so full of mercy for all who ask for Your help.

Psalm 86:5